THE
MYSTERIOUS CASE
CASE

DETERMINED DETECTIVES

THE MYSTERIOUS CASE CASE

by Mary Blount Christian

illustrated by Ellen Eagle

Troll Associates

A TROLL BOOK, published by Troll Associates,
Mahwah, NJ 07430

Text copyright © 1985 by Mary Blount Christian
Illustrations copyright © 1985 by Ellen Eagle

Published by arrangement with E.P. Dutton, a division of
NAL Penguin Inc. For information address E.P. Dutton,
a division of NAL Penguin Inc., 2 Park Avenue,
New York, New York 10016.

First Troll Printing, 1988

Printed in the United States of America.

10 9 8 7 6 5 4 3 2 1

ISBN 0-8167-1311-1

for all those determined detectives
in Mystery Writers of America, southwest chapter,
who are having the crime of their lives

CONTENTS

P Is for Perfect

The *tippity tap tap* of Mary Alice Rodriguez's tap shoes on center stage echoed off the wall behind me. Nervously I drummed my fingers against my clarinet, in time—*tippity tap tap.*

We were in the school auditorium to try out for Scudder Elementary School's Annual Amateur Night. Mrs. Ryder, the principal, was an audience of one. She was going to decide who got to be in the show—and who didn't. I glanced over at my best friend, Gerald Grubbs. He was hanging on to his saxophone as if it might fly away from him. His knuckles were white, he held it so tight.

"When's it going to be our turn, Fenton?" he asked, his voice raspy with fear. He sniffled. Whenever he gets nervous, his nose gets sniffly.

I, Fenton P. Smith, am his hero, so I tried to reassure him. "Mary Alice is almost through," I said. "Then there's that dumb old Mae Donna Dockstadter and her magic act, then us. Don't worry." I forced a smile I didn't feel. "As sure as the *P* in my name is for Perfect, that's what we'll be. Mrs. Ryder can't help but choose us."

I admit, I was getting a little bit antsy myself. As good as we were with our duet, there had already been harmonica, accordion and piano renditions of "Glow Worm," and that was the only piece we knew well enough to play. Besides, I wanted to get the audition over with and get to the library before it closed.

According to the Just Arrived list at the library, there was this new book on the shelves, *Private Eye Handbook,* that I wanted to check out. The librarian had ordered it months ago. I like to keep up with the competition. As half of the team of Smith and Grubbs, Determined Detectives, I blushingly admit there may be a few things we still don't know.

Mary Alice *clip-clop*ed past us, sweat beads lining her upper lip. Then I caught a whiff of lavender behind me. Without turning, I knew that Mae Donna Dockstadter was there. When you are a great detective, you come to know these things. Mae Donna must soak herself in lavender, because she always smells just like my grandmother's guest bathroom.

Mae Donna had a big black cape draped over her shoulders. Her crazy red corkscrew curls sprang out from under a shiny black top hat and bounced as she walked. She glared at me and Gerald with those green cat-eyes of hers before she stuck her nose up in the air and pushed past us. She stopped just short of the stage and threw out some powdered stuff. There was a big *whoosh,* and suddenly the stage was in a puff of smoke. When it cleared, there she was, bowing and strutting around stage, spreading that huge cape like a peacock's tail feathers.

"I am Mae Donna the Magnificent!" she shouted. She waved her hand and suddenly had a bunch of flowers.

"What a pain!" I groaned. "She thinks she's so great. I hope there's a bee in that bouquet." I chuckled at the thought.

"She's pretty good," Gerald said, shoving his bubble gum to the side of his mouth. "Look, she just pulled a bunch of colored handkerchiefs out of the air."

"Big deal," I said. "May she catch a cold to match them! Let's just hope she gets her act over with so we can get to the library before it closes. I want to get started on that book tonight."

Mae Donna finished her act by pulling a stuffed panda bear out of her top hat.

"That's very good, Mae Donna," Mrs. Ryder said, clapping. "Participants will be posted on the bulletin board outside my office tomorrow. Next?"

"Maybe we should have worn our costumes," Gerald said, a look of panic paling his face. "It would've looked better with our costumes!"

"Come on," I said as Mae Donna and her lavender scent scooted past us, her nose tilted skyward. "We don't need gimmicks—just talent."

We stepped toward center stage—that is, I stepped. Gerald tripped over his saxophone and fell toward center stage. While he picked himself up, I wiggled my lips and licked them, placing my clarinet to my mouth. I tapped my foot—one, two, three and four—setting the tempo. We did a pretty fair rendition of "Glow Worm." Except for a couple of obvious bloopers and Gerald's bubble gum getting tangled up in his saxophone, it would've been perfect.

When we finished, I shaded my eyes and squinted past the lights to see Mrs. Ryder taking notes. She looked pleased. I didn't know if it was because she thought we were that good or because we were the last ones to try out.

She told us about posting the winners tomorrow, then stood to leave, shuffling an armload of papers.

"Come on," I yelled to Gerald. We jammed our instruments into their cases and loped to the library.

I scanned the shelves twice, but I couldn't find *Private Eye Handbook.* Maybe it hadn't been put on the shelves yet. I rushed up to the check-out counter.

"Mrs. Brooks!" I said breathlessly. "*Private Eye Handbook*—where is it?"

The librarian smiled at me, shrugging. "Why, Fenton, I'm sorry. Someone just now checked it out." She nodded toward the door.

I should have known from the whiff of lavender left behind. I whirled to see Mae Donna Dockstadter disappearing out the door. She glanced back, a smug grin

stretched across her face. She was carrying *Private Eye Handbook.*

I groaned. As sure as the *P* in my name is for Problem, that girl proved to be the beginning of ours.

P Is for Pest

I stormed up to Mae Donna and sneezed the lavender out of my nose. "We've been waiting for that book for weeks!" I shouted. "You're just taking it to be mean! What does an amateur magician need with a book about detecting?"

She fixed those green eyes squarely on me and pulled the book to her as if she expected a sneak attack or something. "I've decided to broaden my horizons," she said. "I shall combine my talents of keen observation with those of a superb magician and become a great detective"—she squinted, as if daring me—"following in the footsteps of my famous father so to speak."

"Ha!" I challenged. "Your father, a great detective? So how come I never heard of him, huh? How come?" I glared back at her, eye to eye.

"Don't be stupid!" she snapped. Her corkscrew curls bounced around her like a bunch of Slinkies. "He works undercover. And if you'd *heard* of him, he wouldn't be a very *good* detective, *would* he?"

Well, the way she said it, it did seem logical. But I was not about to let dumb old Mae Donna Dockstadter get the best of the situation. "This town isn't big enough for two detective agencies. And we were here first," I challenged.

She raised one rusty-red eyebrow and glared at me with those green eyes as cold as frozen emeralds. Reading from the book, she said, "Well then, what is the first rule of good surveillance?"

"Huh?" Gerald asked, his mouth hanging open.

"She means tailing a suspect," I whispered.

Gerald closed his mouth with a snap. "Yeah, I knew that."

Mae Donna pursed her lips so her freckles all slid together into one big glop. "Thanks to my expertise in magic—my sleight-of-hand tricks, my ability to make people see only what I wish them to see—surveillance is my specialty." She snorted, then stalked off, leaving us in a whirl of lavender.

"'Surveillance is my specialty,'" Gerald mocked. "Her and her fancy words. Why can't she just say *tail* like us *real* detectives?" Gerald sniffled. "Do you really think her father is a famous detective like she says?"

"Famous detectives don't have dumb old pesty daughters like Mae Donna!" I growled. I tried to add a note of cheer. "Maybe Mae Donna will read the whole book tonight and return it to the library tomorrow. She does get good grades in reading class."

We hiked down the sidewalk at a brisk pace. I couldn't get that dumb old Mae Donna out of my mind, though. What if she was telling the truth? What if her father really was a famous detective? With him to advise her and all the instruction in that book—which should be in our hands right now—she could be real competition to us. "I think we should brush up on our skulking techniques tomorrow after school. We'll wear disguises, and the first one spotted is a rotten egg, okay?"

Gerald nodded enthusiastically and blew a big bubble. It popped, and the pink gum stuck to the end of his nose. "Sure. Where'll we meet? At Main and Crawford?"

"Yeah. Under the big clock in front of the City National Bank. Three thirty sharp—" I sniffed. There was a faint scent of lavender. "Mae Donna Dockstadter!" I yelled. "You don't fool me one bit. You are hiding behind one of the trees. Now stop tailing us, you hear?"

She stepped from behind the big oak tree, a look of surprise on her face. "How did you know?" she asked.

I crossed my arms and threw back my head, laughing. "Because I've had a lot more experience than you!" I said. I wasn't about to tell her about her smelly old perfume and give away a trade secret.

She looked a little dejected, but soon recovered enough to glare at me with those green eyes. "We'll just see about that!" she challenged before clomping off down the street.

I stared after her, wondering if she'd heard our

plans. I frowned. I was supposed to be the *tailer,* not the *tailee.* I didn't like the idea that Mae Donna might be behind any old bush or tree, listening to our secret strategies, eavesdropping on our secret plans. I shrugged, pushing her from my mind. As sure as the *P* in my name stood for Professional, we could handle the likes of her.

The next day at school, Gerald and I hurried to the bulletin board outside Mrs. Ryder's office. I searched the list of acts for the Amateur Night. We were on it. So were Mae Donna the Magnificent and Mary Alice Rodriguez. And so were the harmonica, the accordion and the piano acts. In fact, I couldn't think of anybody that tried out that wasn't on the list.

"You were all just so good," Mrs. Ryder said. "I think all of you should be in the show. You boys may get together with the harmonica, piano and accordion and decide among you who will play 'Glow Worm.' The others may choose different pieces." She smiled warmly.

I turned to Gerald. "The others will just have to choose some other piece. We got dibs on 'Glow Worm.' We'll see them at lunch and tell 'em," I said.

We couldn't find the harmonica, piano or accordion at lunch. "I get a bad feeling about this, Gerald," I said, letting my detective instinct take over. "I think they are avoiding us. That's a bad sign."

We found Walter, the harmonica player, after school. He was trying to sneak out the side door. "We got dibs on 'Glow Worm,' " I said in my most intimidating tone of voice.

"Are you kidding?" he asked. "I was countin' on the rest of you playing something different. The only thing I know well enough to play is 'Glow Worm.'"

"We'll figure something out later," I said. Gerald and I had other things to think about right then—like practicing our skulking techniques.

Mae Donna strutted past me juggling *Private Eye Handbook* and *Tricks for Advanced Magicians* in her arms. She sniggered. "What's that in the sack, Fenton —detective disguises?" She marched down the hall, her hair springing like pogo sticks in all directions.

I blushed. What would be worse? Pretending to have disguises in an ordinary brown paper bag, letting her think she was right? Or admitting that I was carrying a couple of peanut butter and jelly sandwiches left over from lunch, which suddenly seemed so unprofessional? I *hated* letting Mae Donna Dockstadter think she was right about *anything*. How did she know we used disguises? Maybe that book was even better than I'd hoped. She'd caught on pretty fast overnight.

After school, I put on an old derby my father used in a college play, a big checked coat with a pillow stuffed inside to take up the slack and a pair of glasses with a rubber nose and moustache already attached. I gathered a couple of other disguises and some granola bars into Grandpa's old briefcase, which he'd given me when he retired. A good detective is always prepared to change looks in case he is discovered.

I shoved our secret codebook into the case and dashed toward the corner of Main and Crawford. It was always crowded about that time of day. You could have a good selection of suspects to practice tailing.

I reached the corner just as the minute hand touched the six. A good detective is always on time. I glanced around. I didn't see Gerald. As I said, a *good* detective is always on time. Gerald is sometimes something else.

I figured I might as well practice skulking by myself. I skittered behind the big blue mailbox, then skedaddled to an alley between buildings, where the shadows were pretty good. I was just skulking to the newspaper box on the street corner when this guy came whizzing out of the bank's doors and slammed right into me.

We both tumbled to the sidewalk in a tangle. My derby flopped over my eyes, and my glasses popped off —moustache and all.

"Excuse me, sir," I said, trying to be polite as I shoved back my derby and replaced my glasses and moustache.

But by that time, I was apologizing to his back. He had already grabbed his briefcase and was climbing into a taxicab without a word of apology. Talk about rude!

Gerald came up just then and helped me to my feet. He was wearing a pair of baggy plaid trousers, a greenish wig and a polka-dot tie.

I clicked my teeth, disgusted. "You call that a good disguise?" I yelled. "A good detective is supposed to blend in with the crowd."

"Heck," he said, helping me up. "I didn't think you'd recognize me that fast."

"You look like an escapee from the circus!" I brushed myself off. "At least nothing's broken," I said.

I picked up my briefcase. It felt heavier. "Oh, my

gosh!" I yelled. "This isn't mine. It's— Hey, mister!" I yelled at the vanishing taxicab.

Suddenly my knees felt weak. "Gerald!" I gasped. "If I have his briefcase, then he has mine! He'll have our secret codebook! He'll know everything. We'll be ruined!"

I was humiliated. A good detective *never* lets his codebook fall into the hands of others. I felt my face growing warm as the red tinged my ears.

Gerald pointed to some little polished-brass letters on the side. "That's a nice case," he said. "The guy'll probably want to get his own back, too. Maybe there's something important in it."

I blushed. I should've spotted those initials myself. After all, I'm a better detective than Gerald. "W. W.," I read. "Probably his initials." A good detective always comes to quick deductions that way.

"Let's take it home," I suggested. "Maybe his name is inside, and we can set up an exchange. My stuff for his."

We hiked to my house and sat down on the porch swing, panting. I tried the latch on the briefcase. It wasn't locked. I was feeling lucky.

I flipped the top open and peered inside. "Oh, my gosh!" I yelled. "Gerald, it's—it's money!" There were thousands and thousands of bills in neat little stacks, all banded and labeled. *Wheeeeeeeeewooo.* I whistled long and low. I let the stacks fall between my fingers and land in a beautiful green pile in the case.

Wheeeeeeeeewooo, Gerald echoed.

Wheeeeeeeeewooo!

14

Gerald and I stared at each other. That *wheeeeeeeee-wooo* didn't belong to either of us. I sniffed. "Mae Donna!" I yelled. "Come out!"

She tromped from behind a big ligustrum bush. Mae Donna looked like a peacock that had just got a good look at his ugly feet. She was obviously disappointed that we had spotted her.

I was embarrassed that dumb old Mae Donna had followed us without my knowing it. But I had worse things to think about right now, like— "What if that guy thinks I stole the money?" I shrieked. "What if he thinks the whole thing was a plan to switch briefcases?"

A horrible thought hit me. "That guy could've told the cops by now! Gerald, I—I'm a wanted man! I'll spend all my best years in prison—for a crime I didn't commit!"

It was Mae Donna who spoke. "Calm down, Fenton. Did your notebook have your name and address in it?"

"No, I don't go around with my name and address in plain English on such sensitive documents. But how did you know that I had—"

"I *knew* you didn't see me surveilling you!" She smirked.

"*Tailing,* Mae Donna," I yelled. "The word is *tailing!*"

She shrugged. "Whatever. At any rate, I saw the whole thing." She shook her head and the red springs spilled into her eyes.

"Then did you get the license number of the taxi?" Gerald asked. "We could ask the driver where he took the man."

Mae Donna slumped in disappointment. She blushed so, her face and hair were the same color.

I could've hugged Gerald. He sure showed up that Mae Donna! Maybe some of my great detective know-how was finally rubbing off on him.

She crossed her arms defiantly. "So how come a guy would carry that much cash around, huh?"

I frowned at her, then at the case. She could have something there. Why wouldn't he just write a check or get a cashier's check or money order? Why would he have thousands and thousands of dollars all banded and counted unless he'd— I felt my blood drain to my toes. He had cash because crooks don't deal in checks and money orders.

Maybe he was the rich husband of some kidnapped woman, and he was getting ready to take that money to ransom her! What would the kidnappers do when they opened up the case and found no money? It would be curtains for the victim. And curtains for the Determined Detectives, too.

Who'd want to hire us when they found out it was our briefcase that had caused the whole terrible mess? The idea was too horrible to think about. Fate couldn't be that cruel to budding young detectives. It had to be something else. Maybe—yeah, maybe— Maybe the guy was a crook. That money was stolen!

"He's a bank robber!" I yelled. "This money is—is hot!" I swallowed hard, feeling liked a treed raccoon. Not only would the cops be looking for me, that guy would be looking for me, too.

"At least he doesn't know what you—the real you—looks like. You had your disguise on and all," Mae Donna offered.

I relaxed, but then I suddenly remembered. "But my glasses and moustache came off. What if he saw what I look like? If he didn't steal that money, he probably gave my description to the cops. If he did steal it, *he'll* be after me! He might be so mad at me that he'll tell the cops that I did it! For that much money, he's probably willing to—to—" I couldn't finish the sentence. It was too scary.

"—to *kill* you for it?" Mae Donna finished, her eyes bugged out like a praying mantis'.

In the distance, I heard a siren howl. It was coming this way. As sure as the *P* in my name stands for Pickle, that was exactly what I was in!

P Is for Panic

The ambulance wailed past us and turned onto Beechnut Street. Only then did I realize I'd been holding my breath. I let it out with a big "Wheeewww!"

"You can say that again!" Gerald said.

I did. "Wheeewww!"

"Maybe you ought to get that money to the sheriff right now," Gerald suggested, "tell him what happened." His eyes were bugged out, sort of froglike. I was touched that Gerald was concerned for me.

"But what if he doesn't believe me? What if he believes I took the money?" I asked. "Besides, we don't know for sure that W. W. stole the money. Maybe he's just a little weird. Maybe he doesn't have any credit cards and carries a lot of cash with him."

Mae Donna was standing there, tapping her foot in that superior manner of hers, as if she had a solution in her pocket.

"What would your famous detective father do in a case like this?" I asked.

"Huh? Oh, uh—" She tapped the freckles on her forehead and narrowed her cat-eyes. "He'd turn the money in to the bank and get a big reward."

By that time, I'd had a chance to think for myself. "I'll turn the money in to the bank and get a big reward," I said.

Mae Donna clicked her teeth at me and snorted.

I glanced at my watch. "The bank will be closed by now," I said.

"So use the night deposit," Gerald suggested, sniffling. He stole a quick look over both shoulders. "Let's get rid of it—right now."

Didn't I wish we could! But the case wouldn't fit in the little deposit slot. Besides, what about the reward? And the publicity? "Hero Detectives Turn Over Money." Once our reputation spread, that could mean more cases for us. "There's nothing to do but keep the money tonight and turn it in tomorrow after school," I said, sighing.

I crossed my heart, spat in the palm of my hand and held it up. "You've both got to swear that you won't say anything about this. If anybody knew I had all this money . . ."

Gerald crossed his heart, spat in the palm of his hand and slapped my hand. We turned to Mae Donna.

"Ick!" she said, wrinkling her nose in distaste. "You'll just have to trust me!"

Gerald shrugged. "So where are you going to hide the money for the night?"

I narrowed my eyes and looked back over my shoulder, then leaned forward, whispering. "It'd go easier on the two of you if you don't know—you know, in case of torture or anything. I'll figure out something. I'll see you tomorrow—er, you too, Mae Donna." I figured I needed all the friends I could get right now. Besides, I thought ahead, we may need her father's advice before this is over.

It was about time for my mom and dad to get home from work, so I cased the house to see where I could stash the dough—that's detective talk.

The vacuum cleaner? Naw. What if Mom got on a cleaning binge and threw out the dust bag filled with money? The freezer? She might decide to quick-thaw something for supper, and we'd have cooked money. And it was already hot!

I rummaged through my old toy box and found a Winnie-the-Pooh pajama bag. I stuffed all the money into Pooh, then set him on my bed where I could keep an eye on him.

That's where I was when Mom called me to supper. "Can I eat in here?" I asked. I smiled at her, trying to look as innocent as possible.

"No way, Fenton," she said. "Supper is the only family time we have together."

Mom's big on family togetherness. She takes all those magazine tests to be sure we're a together family and to "influence my adolescent development through cognitive communication"—in other words, not botch up on raising me. I guess she thinks if I eat alone in my room one night, I might grow up to be a bank robber

21

or something—I got the point. But just to be safe, I carried Pooh along so I could keep an eye on him.

I set him in the fourth chair. Mom and Dad exchanged funny looks. "You feeling all right, Fenton?" Mom asked.

"Sure, Mom." I slurped my vegetable soup. "Wonderful soup, Mom."

"It's canned," she said. "Did you and Gerald have a fight?"

"No, Mom." *Slurp!*

Dad leaned forward and looked over his glasses' rims at me. He frowned and cleared his throat apologetically. "Everything all right at school, son?"

"Fine, Dad." *Slu-u-r-p!*

Mom glanced over at Pooh, then back at me. "Is there *anything* you'd like to discuss, Fenton? I mean, *anything?*"

"Dad's already told me all that stuff, Mom. And we had a film in class. I'm fine, really." *Slur-r-p!*

Mom brought out the spaghetti. She stole glances at me. "Do you think he's feverish?" she asked my dad.

He kept watching me out of the corner of his eye, stopping now and then to shake his head. "You know," he finally said, "when I have a problem at work, sometimes it helps to tell somebody—you know, get their feedback." When I just kept on slurping, he muttered under his breath and concentrated on his plate.

Mom and Dad looked at each other, at me, then at Pooh—if they only knew! I just kept slurping up those little noodles and licking the sauce from my lips. We

had chocolate ice cream for dessert, then I asked to be excused and grabbed Pooh.

Mom pulled me to her. "Fenton, you know your father and I love you very, very much. Maybe we don't tell you that enough, being busy at work and all that. Fenton, is that it? Are you upset because I *work*, because I'm not here when you really *need* me?"

I sighed. I recognized that test from last month's *Model Mother* magazine: "Is Your Child Jealous of Your Job?" We had to take the test together—twice!

"Gee, Mom. You've been working since I was five. I think it is just great. May I be excused please?" Mom kissed me on the forehead—her way of checking to see if I had a temperature. Then Dad shook my hand, opened his mouth to say something, but didn't, then hugged me. I took Pooh to my room, sure that my "problem" would give them a topic of conversation for the rest of the evening.

I pulled out an old school composition book and wrote a secret message to Gerald—just in case. *Money rhymes with honey, Pooh's favorite food.* That should let Gerald know the money is hidden in Pooh's tummy— just in case. I did my homework, practiced "Glow Worm" on the clarinet, then crawled into bed, placing Pooh on the pillow next to me. His stomach crackled with the money.

I listened to the news on my Walkman. The biggest local news was about a bus drivers' strike. It seems the company and the drivers got in a wage dispute, and the drivers walked off the job. It abruptly shut down both the inbound and outbound traffic for the day. There was no mention of a robbery. The bank ought to know if it was robbed, so that left out that theory. There was no mention of a kidnapping, either. Nor did the announcer say that W. W. was looking for an unknown mugger. Why not? Unless he planned to get the money back without the sheriff's help?

The tree branch outside swished in the light breeze and scraped my window. A raccoon *scritch*ed across the roof. Insects slapped against the pane. All these things happen every night. Tonight they all seemed scary.

The door to my room opened a crack. I wrapped my arms around Pooh extra tight. No one was going to get him without a fight.

"It's probably just a new phase," I heard Mom whisper. "I read . . ." The door shut.

Some phase, I thought. Call this my scared-for-my-life phase. What if W. W. was smarter than he looked? What if he were able to unscramble the code and decipher the address?

I would be so glad when this night was over. Somewhere out there in the town was a perpetrator who might be looking for me. *Perpetrator,* I thought sleepily. Mae Donna Dockstadter would like that word. Yuk. W. W. and Mae Donna—two miserable complications to my young and tortured life.

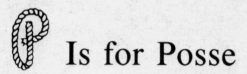 Is for Posse

I must have dropped off to sleep at last, because the next morning I had to be shaken awake by Mom. The alarm clock was blaring away, and I hadn't even heard it.

Mom looked awfully sad. I realized I was hanging on to Pooh with all my might. I guess she thought it was a sign that our family was losing some of its togetherness.

She heaved a sigh and squared her shoulders. "Hurry up and shower and get dressed, or you'll be late to school."

I could already smell the bacon and pancakes—Mom is a firm believer in food being the solution to most problems, so to speak.

I grabbed Pooh in one hand and my clothes in the other and dashed for the bathroom, still steamy and smelling of Dad's after-shave.

While I showered, I thought. I couldn't carry that

dumb bear around school with me. But I couldn't leave the money at home, either. I didn't want to carry W. W.'s briefcase and have kids asking me about that. Then it hit me— What is Fenton P. Smith always carrying? My clarinet!

I gobbled the pancakes and bacon, sloshed down the orange juice and dashed back to my room. I stashed the deflated Pooh and my clarinet in the bottom of my toy box. I stuffed the clarinet case with the money, then waved a quick good-bye to Mom. She looked relieved that I wasn't carrying Pooh. She grinned, probably convinced that bacon and pancakes really did solve the problem.

Gerald was already out on the sidewalk. He raised one eyebrow in a silent question. I patted my clarinet case and winked broadly.

I felt pretty clever at hiding the money until Mae Donna clomped up, red whorls of hair flopping into her face.

"So it's in your clarinet case, huh?" she said, a smug look crossing her face.

I know my jaw must've dropped to the floor, because she shrugged. "Nobody holds a plain old clarinet case that seriously," she said. She crossed her arms smugly. "Of course, nobody else would notice, Fenton, because nobody else knows about the m-o-n-e-y, except us detectives."

I groaned and looked around before answering. "Maybe not, Mae Donna. But all of us here at Scudder Elementary can s-p-e-l-l, for crying out loud!"

She shrugged and tossed her head. The red spirals

did flip-flops. "Whatever. Are you going to the bank right after school?"

I figured she'd want to tag along, so I said, "Naw. I'll wait until just before closing time—so it won't be so crowded, you know. Wouldn't want to cause a riot with all that money." We could go as soon as school was out —without her. Why should we let that detective-come-lately get any credit for our caper? Besides, she might do something to spoil it all.

She narrowed her cat-eyes at me, but she didn't say anything. She just whirled around and stalked off, her sausage curls bouncing around like a deli in an earth-quake.

Somebody yelled, "Hey, Fenton, Gerald, wait up!"

I pulled the clarinet case closer to me, then relaxed, realizing that it was Dexter Pemberton, the accordion player.

"We got a problem," he said.

"Stand in line," I said.

"No, I mean it," he said. "I talked to Alicia, the piano player, and to Walter. It seems that none of us know any pieces but 'Glow Worm.' So now what do we do?"

I wheezed. "Dexter, if that were the extent of my problems, I'd consider myself lucky. Don't worry. We'll figure something out, as sure as the *P* in my name stands for Positive."

He shrugged and trotted off down the hall, wobbling under the weight of his accordion case.

Somehow I made it through the day—under the watchful eyes of Gerald and of course, Mae Donna, who watched us from behind *Private Eye Handbook* most of the time. When the dismissal bell rang, Gerald and I headed for the only place safe from Mae Donna Dockstadter—the boys' room.

We put on our disguises. I had on a spy-type raincoat, a skinlike skullcap that made me look bald and a dark moustache. Gerald had on his baggy pants again. But this time, he wore a curly white wig, a hot-pink and yellow flowered shirt and dark sunglasses. He looked as if he'd just arrived from Hawaii.

I peeked outside and looked in both directions. No one in sight.

I motioned to Gerald, and we trotted down the hall and out of the building. Satisfied that we'd dodged Mae Donna, we headed directly for Main and Crawford.

We took deep breaths, then pushed into the bank. The lobby was empty except for a woman wearing a blue blazer and a bored look on her face. The name plate on her desk said Mazie Greene, Receptionist. She was on the phone.

"Mr. Walker left on vacation yesterday," she said. "Yes, I know it seems strange to leave in the middle of the week, but Walter had a couple of extra days coming. I can let you talk to Mr. Hasselbum, our bank president. He's a little busy preparing for the auditors next week, but I'm sure he'd be glad to help you.

"Oh, this is a personal call? Fine, you can call back in two weeks, then. That's when he'll be back. Goodbye."

She yawned again. "Now, may I help you gentlemen?"

I shoved the case on her desk and opened it. "I have this money—"

Her eyes bugged out. "Ooooooh!" she cooed. "You certainly do! Name?"

I figured she wanted to get my name for the reward money. Maybe she wanted to write a check. "Cash would be best," I said, smiling under my false moustache. I tipped my derby. I didn't want to have my name lying around, just in case that guy tried to come after me.

She nodded. "C-a-s-h. Any kin to that singer?"

I frowned, not understanding.

She shrugged. "First name?"

I decided to use one of my aliases. "John," I lied.

She scowled at me. "Are you sure you're not kin to that singer?" She shrugged and spelled out loud as she typed. "J-o-h-n."

"Address?"

My detective instinct told me this was not going the way I'd planned. I gave her the address of the library.

"Amount of money here?"

I figured she was testing me, to see if I'd sneaked out any, or maybe she just wanted to see if I could count. I'd counted it enough last night, so I squared my shoulders and said, "One million dollars. In stacks of fifty thousand-dollar bills."

She smiled at me, wide-eyed. I could see the stacks of bills reflected in her eyes. She whipped the paper from her typewriter, scooped up the stacks of money and disappeared through a door marked Horace Hasselbum, President.

Gerald and I waited nervously, discussing how much reward we would be getting. This was turning out to be easier than I'd dreamed!

The woman came back in a few minutes without the cash and with her arms loaded with stuff. She shoved a flash camera into my arms—not what I'd expected, but not bad. We could use it in our detective work.

"That's for being our one-thousandth customer this year," she said. She stuffed a box filled with six Mickey Mouse drinking glasses into Gerald's arms. "And this is for being the one-millionth customer in the bank's history. And this," she said, stacking a baseball signed by the entire team of the Scudder Otters on top of the camera, "is for opening such a large account at our bank. Just sign this deposit slip and fill out these forms."

I could feel my jaw drop. "Account?" I yelled. This woman was really confused. "I had better see the president!" I insisted.

I grabbed my empty clarinet case and balanced the camera and baseball in the other hand. Gerald stuck the box of glasses under his arm. We stalked past the woman and into Mr. Hasselbum's office.

He was sitting there running his fingers through the stacks of money, a weird look dancing in his eyes.

I slammed the empty case on his desk, then jammed my free hand in my pocket, to keep it from shaking. "See this empty case?" I began.

The guy's eyes nearly popped out of his head. "Y-y-yes, sir!" he said. He threw a couple of stacks of money into the case.

I frowned and tried again. "I'm *not* trying to open an account here, understand?"

"Oh, y-y-yes sir," he said. "I understand, p-p-perfectly!" He threw another couple of stacks into the case before pushing a red button on his desk.

I doubled my fist in my pocket. "But what about the million dollars?" I yelled.

"Y-y-yes sir," he said. He tossed the rest of the money into the case, wiping sweat from his forehead with the sleeve of his coat.

Then it hit me. This guy thought—he thought we were bank robbers! And that red button on his desk? He'd hit the silent alarm! The sheriff would be here any minute now.

I used my detective's deduction: It would be healthier to get out of here now and explain later!

I grabbed the case with one hand and Gerald's arm with the other. He managed to grab the baseball and camera while giving me a puzzled look.

There was a big commotion as the sheriff burst into the office, waving his gun in the air. By this time, even Gerald had tumbled to what was going on. He and I tore out the alley door, setting off a loud bell.

"Run!" I screamed at Gerald. "Run for your life!"

The sheriff was right behind us down the alley and was inches away from nabbing the back of my coat collar when suddenly a dumpy old bag lady stepped from behind two shipping boxes. She tossed some powdered stuff into the air, and there was a flash of blinding smoke.

P Is for Problem

I felt my derby being snatched from my head, then my glasses—moustache and all—and finally my coat. I flailed, yelling, "I didn't do it! It's a mistake!"

"Shut up, Fenton! It's me!"

I was shoved to a sitting position on the sidewalk.

I got a whiff of lavender. As the smoke cleared, there was Mae Donna, corkscrew curls bouncing, sitting next to me and Gerald. Beside her was a well-stuffed bag, containing, no doubt, my and Gerald's disguises as well as one for a dumpy bag lady.

The sheriff stumbled forward, waving away the last puff of smoke. "You kids see the Scudder Halloween Bandits run this way?"

Mae Donna looked up at him, her green eyes as cool as anything. "They went that way," she said, pointing and smiling innocently.

"Thanks," he said. He waved to his deputy, and the two of them leaped into their black and white and careened down the street, siren blasting away.

"Thanks," I said. "But how—"

"Magician's secret," she said, nodding the direction we should walk—opposite the sheriff and his deputy. "I take it your idea to return the money didn't work out exactly the way you planned."

"You can say that again," Gerald said.

"It's weird," I said. "I mean, if that guy hasn't reported that the money was stolen from him, it *has* to be because he stole it in the first place. He *must* have taken it from the City National Bank because he was coming out of there with the money. So why doesn't the bank know it's been robbed?"

"It knows now!" Gerald reminded me.

"Scudder Halloween Bandits, indeed!" I snorted. "How did he ever come up with a dumb name like that?"

We came to a dusty-green house with pink roses in front. A man with freckles and tight red curls was mowing the lawn. He waved.

My detective instincts took over. "That your dad?" I asked Mae Donna. Gosh, I have to mow our lawn every Saturday. Somehow I'd hoped, when I became a great detective, that I'd be above such menial labor. But maybe he finds that relaxing after a hard day of chasing criminals. Then again, I guess it beats growing orchids like that fat detective Nero Wolfe.

We went through the white picket fence, and he shut off the mower.

"You're Fenley, and you must be Jeremy," he said, extending his hand.

"Fenton and Gerald," I said, figuring he was using some clever detective device to draw us out. I made a mental note to use it sometimes—pretend ignorance.

"Having fun?" he asked, grinning.

"Loads," I said. "May I ask you a question, sir? I'd like to follow in your footsteps someday, sir. Would you give me any hints that I could use?"

Mae Donna groaned and turned a bright red. I guess she wanted to keep all her father's good ideas to herself. But after all, she still had *Private Eye Handbook*. Why should she have an exclusive on her father, too?

Mr. Dockstadter nodded. "Why, I'm flattered! Not many boys your age think about going into my line of business!"

"Are you kidding?" I asked. "Why, that's all I've ever wanted to be. Gerald, too!"

"Well, well," he said. "Well, Fenley, I look at it this way. Leave no stone, no rock, no crevice unchecked. Never rest until our homes, our neighborhoods are safe from the vermin and insects that threaten us." He squared his shoulders proudly.

I saluted. "Yes sir! No stone, no rock, no crevice unchecked. I'll remember that, sir!"

Mae Donna had slumped to the steps and buried her head in her folded arms. She groaned again. "I think I hear Mom calling you," she said.

Mr. Dockstadter nodded. "Fenley? Jeremy? Nice to meet you boys. I'll look forward to your competition

someday." He trotted up the steps and disappeared into the house.

"Gee," I said. "He's right, you know."

"He is?" Mae Donna asked. She looked puzzled.

"Of course!" I insisted. "No stone, no rock, no crevice! We've given up on this too easily. We need to work on this case step-by-step, just like Mr. Dockstadter would do it! Think, Gerald. Think, Mae Donna!"

"You start," Mae Donna challenged me.

"Let's think this thing through from the beginning, okay?" I answered. "Stone, rock, crevice. First, W. W. comes barrelling out of the bank so fast, he knocks me down and accidentally takes the wrong briefcase—"

"The one with our secret codebook and granola bars," Gerald interrupted.

I gave him a dirty look and continued. "He doesn't report the money stolen. Why? Because he can't afford to—he stole it."

"So why doesn't the bank know it was robbed?" Mae Donna asked.

"Good question!" I said. I knew it was a good question because I'd asked it earlier, myself. "That's another rock to turn over. Why doesn't the bank know it's— I've got it! Because there is more than one way to rob a bank! You don't have to do it at gunpoint. You can sneak it out! Emb—em—"

"Embezzle?" Mae Donna asked. Her eyes were starting to glitter. "You mean somebody that works for the bank robbed it?"

"Exactly!" I yelled. "W. W.! Walter Walker—that

insect! That vermin!" I said, remembering Mr. Dock-stadter's advice.

"Will you stop talking like that, for crying out loud?" Mae Donna yelled. "Besides, who's Walter Walker?"

Gerald was getting wiggly. I could tell he was getting the idea, too. I squared my shoulders proudly. All my patient teaching was paying off. My assistant was learning his lessons well. "You take it from here," I said. I mean, a teacher has to know when to step back and let the pupil try it on his own.

"While we were in the bank, the receptionist said a bank employee named Walter Walker had left on vacation yesterday. So they wouldn't be suspicious about him until he didn't show up two weeks from now."

I nodded eagerly. "And she also said something about the auditors coming next week. So they wouldn't learn about the robbery until then. By that time, W. W. could be in Brazil or maybe on one of those little islands in the Caribbean! He could be living like a king!"

Gerald blinked. I could tell I had lost him on that thought.

"Why there?" he asked.

"Because they don't have an agreement with the United States to turn our criminals over to us—you know, extradition," I explained. Sometimes my breadth of knowledge astounds even me.

"He could live like a king, and *you* guys could be hunted criminals," Mae Donna added.

I suddenly felt sick at my stomach. She was right.

"Hey, wait!" I yelled, remembering something. "He can't have left town yet—remember? He left in a *taxicab*. That probably means he doesn't have a car."

Mae Donna grinned so her jillions of freckles melted into one big one. "And there's only one other way out of a town the size of Scudder, and that's the bus station!"

"On strike!" I said, pleased that I knew something she didn't know.

"Not anymore!" she said, crossing her arms and pulling her chin up about two inches.

Gerald jumped up and down. "And I remember the schedules, just like we practiced them, too! Remember, Fenton? You said a good detective knows stuff like that off the top of his head. There're southbound buses out of here every evening, so if he couldn't leave yesterday, then he'll be leaving today!"

"Southbound?" I repeated. "Why southbound?"

Gerald looked at me, stunned. "Why, because the southbound bus would go to the international airport. Wouldn't he want to get out of the States the quickest way possible?"

"Of course," I said, recovering enough to look superior. "I was just testing to see if you knew that. Good work, Gerald." I glanced at my watch. "He may not have left yesterday. But he will be leaving in an hour if we don't stop him!" I yelled.

Since we weren't far from the bus station, we dashed into Mae Donna's house and called the sheriff. I told him just enough to get him there.

Then we jogged to my house to get W. W.'s briefcase and stuff it with the money. I had a plan. If it worked, we'd be free and that guy would be carted off to jail.

If it didn't . . .

Well, it had just *better* work!

P Is for Plan

My breath was coming in quick, hard pants, and my ribs ached, but I still ran. I could hear Gerald and Mae Donna right behind me. The bus station was just ahead of me. In the distance, a siren sounded. It had to be the sheriff in his black and white. If he got there before I pulled off my plan, the guy would look innocent, and I'd still be stuck with the hot money. What I needed now was perfect timing—and a little luck.

I came to a quick stop just inside the bus station. Gerald and Mae Donna didn't stop quick enough, and they collided with me—*oof!*

"Do you see him?" Mae Donna whispered, breathing heavily. "Were we right? Is he here?"

I wheezed a sigh of relief. I was right. There he was, pulling my briefcase out of a rental locker. He probably stored it yesterday when he found out about the bus strike. He must have shoved it into the locker without even looking at it. He didn't know about the switch. He was holding it as if he thought it had a million dollars in it instead of a secret codebook and granola bars.

I realized I was going to have to be awfully clever. But then, that's one of my primary reasons for being a detective—being awfully clever.

The siren was a lot closer now. Then it shut off. My guess was the black and white was only about a block away, and the sheriff was shutting off the siren so he wouldn't scare away the suspect.

"Wait here," I told Gerald and Mae Donna. "And be ready for anything, okay?"

They nodded and I aimed myself at the guy, closed my eyes and ran forward at top speed. *Whammo!* I ran smack into him, and the two of us tumbled to the floor in a tangle of legs and briefcases. It was like an instant replay of yesterday.

I shoved his briefcase toward him. "Excuse me, sir!" I apologized. "I should watch where I'm going next time."

He growled at me and grabbed his briefcase just as the sheriff and his deputy dashed into the bus station.

The guy took one look at the sheriff and paled. He started easing away from the line, backing toward the rear exit—slowly, so he wouldn't catch the sheriff's attention.

In a flash Mae Donna and Gerald dashed across the lobby, screaming at the top of their lungs.

"Daddy, Daddy, please don't desert your darling children here in this lonely bus station! Please take us with you!" Mae Donna yelled.

People turned and gave him dirty looks. A couple of the bigger guys edged toward him, telling him what they thought of guys who would desert their kids in a bus station.

About that time, Mae Donna whipped out some of her magic dust and—*poof!*—W. W. disappeared for a second inside a puff of smoke, yelling words I won't repeat here.

"There he is, sheriff!" I yelled. "That's the man you want!" I could see Mae Donna and Gerald weren't heavy enough to hold him down, so I ran over and sat on the guy's stomach too.

The sheriff and his deputy scrambled over to the pile of people and helped everyone to their feet. The sheriff scratched his head. "But there were *two* Scudder Halloween Bandits—and according to the description Hasselbum and his receptionist gave, they were a whole lot shorter!"

"Look in the briefcase!" I yelled. "There's the stolen money!"

Walter Walker broke out in a sweat, then suddenly shoved his briefcase toward me. "This belongs to him!" he said. "He knocked me down. He must've switched briefcases with me. Isn't that right, folks?" He turned to the crowd of onlookers.

They all nodded yes, and there I was—left holding the briefcase with the million dollars in it. I could see

myself going off to jail and my mom believing it was because she'd failed some dumb magazine test. "Gerald! Mae Donna! Help!" I wailed. "Tell the sheriff I'm innocent!"

Mae Donna stepped forward, shoving the whorls of red curls from her eyes. "This can all be settled quite simply, sheriff," she said. "There are two briefcases here —basically alike, right? Only one has a million dollars in stolen cash in it, and the initials W. W. on it. The other has a notebook with childish scribblings and a couple of granola bars. Now, I ask you sheriff, which briefcase would a man in a three-piece blue suit, on his way out of town, be carrying?"

I growled at Mae Donna. "What do you mean the secret codebook for the Determined Detectives is childish scribblings?" I swallowed hard and turned toward the sheriff. "My name is Fenton P. Smith," I said. "This man is Walter Walker. Who would be more likely to carry a briefcase with the initials W. W. on it?" I glared at Mae Donna, letting her know that *my* logic was better—and not half as *embarrassing*.

She shrugged. "Whatever."

The sheriff took us all to the station to sort the whole thing out in what he said would be a more peaceful atmosphere. By the time we had explained to him how the robbery had taken place and how we happened to be in the middle of it, the sheriff had himself a good laugh and W. W. had himself a good lawyer.

Gerald, Mae Donna and I got our pictures in the paper, the big stack of money in front of us. We didn't get the reward we'd expected from the bank, but Mr. Hasselbum said we could keep the camera, the Mickey Mouse glasses and the signed baseball. He said he'd probably need the reward money for advertising. He said he had to restore people's confidence in the bank again after they read how he'd handed over all that money to a couple of kids in costumes. That and how he didn't even know he'd been robbed in the first place!

Mae Donna turned *Private Eye Handbook* into the library, and I checked it out. It had some good stuff in it, but nothing quite so helpful as the expert advice from Mr. Dockstadter. I would always remember his formula for a successful detective: Leave no stone, no rock, no crevice unchecked. That just about says it all.

Walter, Dexter, Alicia, Gerald and I finally solved our problem with "Glow Worm" to Mrs. Ryder's satisfaction. For Scudder Elementary School's Amateur Night, we were a quintet—clarinet, saxophone, piano, accordion and harmonica. Nobody seemed to mind that we were all playing in different keys. Maybe that was because our playing together cut three music acts from the show.

Mom was especially happy because she figured I was "relating well to my peers." I'd stuffed Pooh back into the corner of the toy box, which must have reassured her, too.

After the show, Gerald and I spotted Mr. Dockstadter. He was backstage helping Mae Donna with all her magic props. Over her objections, Gerald and I offered to help him carry all the junk to their car.

I nearly dropped my end of the disappearing-person box when we came to their big van. It said: Dockstadter, Exterminator/No Stone Unchecked.

Mae Donna narrowed her cat-eyes at me defiantly. "You expect him to drive around in something that says Private Eye on it?" she snarled. "What better disguise for a great detective?"

I thought about that. It seemed logical enough. I made a mental note: Exterminators can get into places without arousing suspicion.

Mae Donna flashed a smug smile. "Now that you have completed your perusal of *Private Eye Handbook,* I suppose you are better prepared for our next surveillance." Her eyes glistened like lime lollypops.

"It's *tail,* Mae Donna. Not surveillance, *tail,* " I said.

She shrugged. "Whatever."

"Besides, there is no you, Gerald and me. It's just Gerald and me." I glared at her, just so there'd be no misunderstanding. If her own father didn't let her detect for him, why should we?

She stuck her nose in the air, wheeled around and, leaving a vapor trail of lavender, she clomped off in a huff.

I had the distinct feeling we hadn't heard the last from that pesky old Mae Donna Dockstadter. But we could cope with her interference as sure as the *P* in my name stands for Perseverance. After all, we were the Determined Detectives!

MARY BLOUNT CHRISTIAN says, "Fenton P. Smith is the kind of kid I was. I loved disguises and I got totally involved in my make-believe projects, and my playmates sort of went along, humoring me. But then there was this one kid who didn't play the game right—she looked amazingly like Mae Donna!"

Mrs. Christian is the author of many books, including the Sebastian (Super Sleuth) mysteries. She lives in Houston, Texas.

ELLEN EAGLE illustrated *Gertie's Green Thumb* by Catherine Dexter and *Supermouse* by Jean Ure. She lives in Glen Ridge, New Jersey.